Even the Smallest will grow

Lita Judge

A Atheneum Books for Young Readers
atheneum New York London Toronto Sydney New Delhi

Tucked beneath a blanket of leaves,
the acorn sleeps until its roots are ready to reach
deep into the earth,
and it begins to grow . . .

just as you,
  stretching your toes under warm sheets
    and resting your head on a dream-filled pillow,
      will grow.

Patience, little one.
There is strength in even the smallest things.

A tadpole waits for tiny buds
to lengthen into legs

so he can hop away.

A newborn calf drinks her
mother's rich milk

until she grows big enough
to swim around the world.

You too will grow.
What will you become?

Will you be an artist,
like the tiniest seed

that blossoms into a flower,
painting color into the world?

Or will you be a poet,
like the seashell that grows in spirals

until his depths hold a secret song?

Will you be a seeker,
like the bird that silently grows
within her egg

until she hatches and flies away
to explore land, sea, and sky?

Or will you be mighty,
like the clouds that deepen
and strengthen into a storm?

You can grow to be anything you want.

You can be sleek and fast,
like the horse
that once was a wobble-legged foal.

You can be curious,
like the giraffe
that must have once felt like
the smallest creature ever born,

or loving and loyal,
like the koala
that holds her baby tight.

You can be fierce and brave,
like the bear
that began as a tiny cub
safely hidden within a cozy den.

Now you are small.
But just as the acorn takes its time
to sprout into an oak,
you will take the time *you* need
to become anything you want.

Remember, little one . . .

even the smallest will grow.

For Pulina

ATHENEUM BOOKS FOR YOUNG READERS • An imprint of Simon & Schuster Children's Publishing Division • 1230 Avenue of the Americas, New York, New York 10020 • Copyright © 2021 by Lita Judge • All rights reserved, including the right of reproduction in whole or in part in any form. • ATHENEUM BOOKS FOR YOUNG READERS is a registered trademark of Simon & Schuster, Inc. Atheneum logo is a trademark of Simon & Schuster, Inc. • For information about special discounts for bulk purchases, please contact Simon & Schuster Special Sales at 1-866-506-1949 or business@simonandschuster.com. • The Simon & Schuster Speakers Bureau can bring authors to your live event. For more information or to book an event, contact the Simon & Schuster Speakers Bureau at 1-866-248-3049 or visit our website at www.simonspeakers.com. • Book design by Sonia Chaghatzbanian and Karyn Lee • The text for this book was set in Museo 300. • The illustrations for this book were rendered in pencil, watercolor, and digitally. • Manufactured in China • 0121 SCP • First Edition • 10 9 8 7 6 5 4 3 2 1 • Library of Congress Cataloging-in-Publication Data • Names: Judge, Lita, author, illustrator. • Title: Even the smallest will grow / Lita Judge. • Description: First edition. | New York City : Atheneum Books for Young Readers, [2021] | Audience: Ages 4–8. | Audience: Grades K–1. | Summary: At bedtime, a mother uses images from nature to tell her daughter that she will grow to become anything she wants to be, although it will take time. • Identifiers: LCCN 2019031831 | ISBN 9781534457256 (hardcover) | ISBN 9781534457263 (eBook) • Subjects: CYAC: Growth—Fiction. | Nature—Fiction. | Mothers and daughters—Fiction. | Bedtime—Fiction. • Classification: LCC PZ7.J894 Eve 2021 | DDC [E]—dc23 • LC record available at https://lccn.loc.gov/2019031831